Rihanna
the Seahorse
Fairy

Special thanks to Narinder Dhami

ISBN 978-0-545-42599-5

12 11 10 9 8 7 6 5 4 3 2 1   12 13 14 15 16/0

Printed in the U.S.A.   40

First Scholastic printing, February 2012

Rihanna
the Seahorse
Fairy

by Daisy Meadows

SCHOLASTIC INC.

New York   Toronto   London   Auckland

Sydney   Mexico City   New Delhi   Hong Kong

There are seven special animals,
Who live in Fairyland.
They use their magic powers
To help others where they can.

A dragon, black cat, phoenix,
A seahorse, and snow swan, too,
A unicorn and ice bear—
I know just what to do.

I'll lock them in my castle
And never let them out.
The world will turn more miserable,
Of that, I have no doubt!

Contents

Adventure Lake

"Oh, I'm really looking forward to going canoeing again!" Kirsty Tate said eagerly to her best friend, Rachel Walker. The girls were carrying a lightweight canoe on their shoulders as they walked through the camp toward Adventure Lake. "But I'm going to try to keep my feet dry this time!"

Rachel laughed. "Yes, it's a lot of fun, isn't it?" she agreed. "I'm glad we have some free time this afternoon so that we can have another try."

"We're not just here to have fun though, are we?" Kirsty added, glancing around to check that none of the other campers were close enough to hear. "We're trying to help our fairy friends, too!"

On the day the girls arrived at the adventure camp, the king and queen of Fairyland had asked for their help to find seven missing magical animals. These special young animals had amazing powers that helped to spread

the kind of magic that humans and
fairies could possess — the wonderful
gifts of imagination, good luck, humor,
friendship, compassion,
healing, and courage.

The seven Magical
Animal Fairies
spent a whole
year training them
before the animals
returned to their
families in Fairyland.
At that time, they were
ready to use their special
talents to help everyone in both
the human and the fairy worlds.
However, spiteful Jack Frost was
determined to put a stop to all this,
simply because he wanted everyone to

be as lonely and miserable
as he was. So he
and his goblins
had kidnapped the
magical animals and
taken them to his
Ice Castle. But the
animals had managed to escape,
and now they were hiding in the
human world! Rachel and Kirsty were
determined to find all seven magical
animals before Jack Frost and his goblins
did. Then the girls planned to return
them safely to Fairyland.

"We've done pretty well so far, haven't
we, Kirsty?" Rachel remarked. "We've
found Ashley's dragon, Lara's black cat,
and Erin's phoenix."

Kirsty nodded. "I just hope we find the

others before the end of the week—"
she began.
But just then
Lila, one of
the camp
counselors, came
out of a nearby
tent. Kirsty and
Rachel exchanged
a warning glance.

Both girls knew that no one in the
human world could ever find out about
the existence of fairies.

"Ah, I see you're off to Adventure
Lake," Lila remarked with a smile.
"Don't forget to put your life jackets on,
OK? And if you need any help, there
are always lots of counselors around
the lake."

"OK, Lila," Kirsty replied. "We'll be careful."

"Well, the secret to fun and successful canoeing is teamwork," Lila said, with a twinkle in her eye. "So you two should be marvelous at it because you're such good friends!"

Kirsty and Rachel grinned at each other as Lila headed off.

"Not just good friends," Rachel laughed. "*Best* friends!"

Adventure Lake lay at the edge of the camp. The surface of the water rippled and shimmered in the sunlight.

Carefully, Rachel and Kirsty set the canoe down at the water's edge and began to put on their life jackets. As they did, Catherine, one of their bunkmates, came running up to them.

"Hey, you guys!" she cried, smiling happily. "Guess what? I just passed my swimming test!"

"Good job!" Kirsty said warmly.

"That's great, Catherine," Rachel agreed. "What are you doing for the rest of free time? Do you want to ride in the canoe with us?"

Catherine shook her head. "Thanks, but I'm going swimming with Emma, Natasha, and Katie," she replied. "Now that I've passed my test, I'm allowed to swim out to the end of the floating

dock." She pointed at the wooden dock that led from the shore out into the lake. The rest of their bunkmates were already splashing around  there and shrieking with laughter.

"Are you two coming to craft time later?" Catherine went on. "I think we're making friendship bracelets."

"We definitely won't miss that!" Kirsty laughed. "We want to make friendship bracelets for you and all the other girls in our cabin."

"I think you'll both get lots of bracelets back in return!" Catherine said with a grin. "Have a good time canoeing. By the way"—she winked at Rachel and Kirsty— "you'd better watch out for the mythical creature that lives at the bottom of the lake!"

Rachel and Kirsty glanced at each

other in shock. *What mythical creature was Catherine talking about?* Kirsty wondered, confused. Could it be one of the magical animals she and Rachel were searching for? And how did Catherine know? Everything about Fairyland was supposed to be a secret!

Catherine laughed. "Don't look so serious, you guys!" she teased. "The lake creature is just an old legend, that's all. See you later!" And she ran off.

"Phew, I was worried there for a minute!" Rachel whispered to Kirsty, looking relieved as they climbed into the canoe.

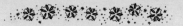

"Me, too!" Kirsty replied, settling herself into the front seat. "Ready, Rachel?"

They pushed themselves away from the bank with their paddles, and then set off across the water, rowing smoothly and rhythmically. The girls could see bright blue dragonflies skimming across the surface of the lake. There were lots of ducks quacking loudly and occasionally dipping their heads underwater.

As Rachel and Kirsty passed by the floating dock, they waved at their friends and then paddled on.

"There are lots of campers enjoying the water today," Rachel remarked, spotting several other girls in boats, canoes, and kayaks. "Should we row across to the other bank, Kirsty?"

Kirsty nodded. When they eventually approached the opposite bank, she noticed a crescent-shaped cove among the rocks.

"Look, Rachel!" Kirsty pointed at the entrance to the cove. "Let's explore it!"

"OK," Rachel agreed, "But don't forget we have to be back at camp for craft time."

"Oh, we've got plenty of time," Kirsty replied.

The girls rowed up to the entrance of the cove and peeked inside.

"I can hear splashing," Rachel said, her eyes wide with excitement. "Let's follow the cove all the way around, Kirsty—that splashing noise might be a waterfall!"

Kirsty shook her head. "I changed my mind," she said with a shrug. "The cove's OK, but I want to row around the rest of the lake."

"That's *boring*!" Rachel complained. "I want to explore the cove!"

"No way!" Kirsty snapped, turning

around to glare at Rachel.

"Why do we have to do what *you* want?" Rachel asked crossly.

Suddenly the girls stared at each other in shock. They hardly ever argued!

"Sorry, Rachel," Kirsty blurted. "I don't know what came over me!"

"I'm sorry, too!" Rachel gasped, looking very ashamed. Both girls put their paddles down and hugged each other.

Rachel sighed. "That was horrible—I never want to argue with you again, Kirsty!"

"Me neither," Kirsty agreed. "Look,

we have just enough time to explore the cove *and* the rest of the lake."

"Good idea," Rachel agreed.

The girls swiftly paddled into the cove. As they rounded the curve, Kirsty spotted another canoe just ahead of them. She frowned as she stared at the little boat. The three passengers looked very familiar!

"Rachel!" Kirsty whispered urgently. "Goblins!"

Goblin Fishermen

Rachel peeked over Kirsty's shoulder, and her heart sank when she saw three goblins sitting in the canoe. They were holding a large fishing net.

"They must think one of the magical animals is hiding in the lake!" Kirsty whispered.

"Quick, we can't let them see us!"

Rachel replied in a low voice.

The girls paddled swiftly and silently toward a nearby inlet. They safely tied the canoe to a post and then slipped down inside it, out of sight.

"I wonder which of the magical animals is in the lake?" Rachel murmured, as they peered carefully over the edge of the canoe.

The goblins were each holding a corner of the net, ready to throw it into the water.

"NOW!" shouted the biggest goblin.

The goblins tried to toss the net into the water.

Instead, the breeze blew it back at them, and they all got tangled up. The goblins shrieked with fury as their boat rocked violently from side to side.

"Help!" shouted the smallest goblin as he almost went overboard. He flung out his arms, trying to steady himself, and hit the biggest goblin right on the nose.

"I'll get you for that!" the biggest goblin yelled, lunging at him. But his foot got caught in the net, pitching him forward so that he head-butted the third goblin in the stomach.

"*Ow,* that hurt!" the third goblin roared angrily.

The three goblins glared at each other, clenching their fists. But then, to Kirsty and Rachel's surprise, the smallest goblin stepped forward, smiling apologetically.

"Please forgive me," he said politely. "That was all my fault."

"No, no," the biggest goblin interrupted quickly, "*I* was to blame."

"Ah, time for a group hug!" said the third goblin. Rachel and Kirsty were astonished when the goblins huddled together and put their arms lovingly around one another!

"This is weird!" Rachel whispered.

"Why are the goblins being so nice to one another?"

"I don't know," Kirsty replied, as the goblins gathered up the net again and threw it into the water. "Let's keep watching!"

The goblins waited a moment and then began pulling the net in again.

"We caught something!" the biggest goblin shrieked triumphantly. He pulled a wriggly silver fish from the net and held it up. "Is this a seahorse?"

"No, but good job, anyway!" the smallest goblin said kindly.

The big goblin threw the fish back

into the lake. Then he rummaged in the net again and held up an old, battered boot. "Well, is *this* a seahorse?"

The other goblins shook their heads. "No seahorses here!" they both said, staring down at the net.

Rachel frowned, looking confused. "Kirsty, seahorses don't live in lakes," she whispered. "They're only found in the sea. They need salt water to survive."

"The goblins must be looking for Rihanna's magic seahorse!" Kirsty pointed out excitedly. "A magic seahorse would be able to live *anywhere!*"

"Oh, of course!" Rachel gasped. "The magic seahorse's special power is the gift of friendship. That must be why the goblins are being so nice to one another!"

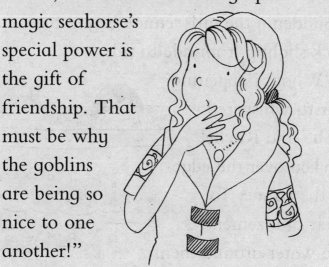

"And remember that the young animals aren't always in control of their magic powers because they're still being trained," Kirsty reminded her. "Their magic can sometimes work in

reverse—and that must be why we argued with each other a little earlier!"

"So the magic seahorse is definitely around here somewhere!" Rachel exclaimed.

Suddenly the girls' canoe began to rock slightly from side to side.

"What's happening?" Kirsty whispered.

She and Rachel peeked over the edge of the canoe. To their amazement, the water around them was filled with sparkling, rainbow-colored bubbles that were causing their canoe to sway gently.

"It's magic!" Rachel gasped, as the bubbles swirled around them. "Do you

think there really *is* a mythical creature in the lake?"

"Or maybe it's the magic seahorse!" Kirsty suggested. "But how are we going to find him before the goblins do? We don't have a fishing net!"

Suddenly a stream of bubbles shot up into the air. A second later, a tiny fairy burst from the water with a shimmering splash, and hovered in the air above Rachel and Kirsty!

Underwater Magic

"Hello, Kirsty and Rachel!" the fairy called, casting a wary glance at the goblins as she floated down toward the girls' canoe. She had long blond hair in flowing waves, and she wore a sea-green dress with a beaded hem. "I'm Rihanna the Seahorse Fairy!"

"Oh, Rihanna, it's great to see you!"

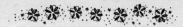

Kirsty cried with a huge smile. "We think your magic seahorse is right here in this lake!"

"But we're not sure how to find him," Rachel added. She pointed at the other canoe. "The goblins are after him, too!"

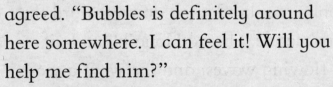

Rihanna nodded. "You're right, girls," she agreed. "Bubbles is definitely around here somewhere. I can feel it! Will you help me find him?"

"Of course we will," Kirsty said eagerly, "but how?"

Their discussion was interrupted by

loud yells from the goblins' canoe as
they pulled the net in again.

"This isn't working!" the smallest
goblin complained,
taking another fish
out and tossing it
back into the lake.

"Let's go
and search
under the water
then," the big goblin suggested.

"How?" the third goblin said with a
shrug. "We can't breathe underwater!"

Rachel, Kirsty, and Rihanna
watched as the big goblin bent down
and pulled something out from under
one of the seats.

"We can use magic to help us!" he
said, waving an ice wand in the air.

29

The other goblins looked astonished.

"Where did you get *that*?" the smallest goblin demanded.

"Jack Frost gave it to me for emergencies," the big goblin replied. "Now that those fairies have returned three of the magical animals to Fairyland, he didn't want to take any chances! We can't let them find any more!"

Rachel, Kirsty, and Rihanna stared at each other in dismay.

"So why haven't we used the wand before?" asked the third goblin with a frown.

The big goblin looked sheepish. "I forgot I had it," he mumbled, shuffling his feet.

The other two goblins glared at him in disgust. For a moment, Kirsty thought they were going to start a fight over the wand, but then the smallest goblin shrugged.

"Let's just get on with it," he said politely. "OK?"

"OK!" said the other two.

"My seahorse's magic is making them be nice to one another!" Rihanna whispered as the goblins began folding  up the fishing net. "Girls, we *have* to find Bubbles before the goblins do. And you'll be able to swim faster if you're fairies like me!"

A flick of Rihanna's wand sent a shower of fairy sparkles drifting around Rachel and Kirsty. Immediately, they shrank until they were as small as

Rihanna herself, with the same sheer
wings on their backs.

"The canoe suddenly seems huge!"
Rachel laughed,
glancing around.

Rihanna lifted her
wand again. This
time, two shiny
bubbles streamed through
the air toward Rachel
and Kirsty. The girls
felt the bubbles settle
over their heads, and
then burst with a pop.

"Now you'll be able to
breathe underwater, just like
when you had your adventure with
Shannon the Ocean Fairy," Rihanna
reminded them. "Let's go!"

Rachel, Kirsty, and Rihanna fluttered over the side of the canoe. They were just about to dive into the water when there was a shout from the goblins.

"Look! Fairies!"

Dismayed, the girls and Rihanna glanced around. They'd been spotted! They saw the big goblin wave the ice

wand at his friends, and goggles and
flippers magically appeared on their
heads and feet.

"Quick, girls!"
Rihanna shouted.

The three friends
plunged into the
waters of the lake.
It was a little
chilly and both
Kirsty and Rachel
gasped as they sank
lower. Schools of
tiny fish wove their
way past the girls.
The bottom of the
lake was carpeted with beautiful green
plants, their leaves waving gently in the
rippling water.

"I didn't realize there was so much going on under the surface!" Kirsty said, as a little frog swam past them.

"It's just as exciting down here as it is on land!" Rachel added. She laughed as a duck floating above them stuck his head underwater and stared at her in surprise.

"I think we should swim westward, girls," Rihanna called. "I'm not sure, but I have a feeling we may find Bubbles in that direction."

"I wonder where the goblins are?" Kirsty remarked as they followed Rihanna to the west. "Let's hope they went eastward!"

Rachel, Kirsty, and Rihanna began to search for the missing seahorse among the plants at the bottom of the lake. But it was hard work. The lake was huge, and the water was very cloudy, making it difficult to see very far ahead. Rachel and Kirsty both began to feel downhearted. How would they ever find Bubbles before the goblins did?

"Girls, I have an idea!" Rihanna

announced, treading her wings in the water. "I have a friend who lives here in the deepest part of the lake's underwater canyon. I think he'll be able to help us find Bubbles more quickly!"

"Oh, I hope so!" Kirsty said eagerly.

Rihanna began to sing:

This is a special message
Rihanna sends to you,
We need your help,
We need it fast,
Please don't delay,
Come right away!

"Charlie!" Rihanna called when she had finished her song. "Charlie, where are you?"

Rachel and Kirsty exchanged a confused look as the water around them began to fizz and bubble.

Who was this mysterious creature named Charlie?

Leggy Garden!

Suddenly, Rachel grabbed Kirsty's arm.

"Look!" she cried.

A large shape, the color of an elephant, was swimming toward them through the bubbles. The strange creature had a long neck and a humped back.

"What *is* it?" Kirsty whispered. "It looks kind of like pictures I've seen of the Loch Ness Monster!"

"Charlie!" Rihanna called, waving at the creature. "Over here!"

Charlie was smiling warmly at them as he swam closer. Rachel was relieved, because otherwise she might have been extremely scared of him. Charlie was so big!

"Girls, this is my friend Charlie," Rihanna announced with a grin. "He's lived in the lake for years. In fact, people tell stories about him, although no human has ever really seen him."

"Oh!" Rachel gasped. "Charlie must

be the mythical creature that Catherine was talking about!"

Rihanna nodded, her eyes twinkling. "Charlie is actually a retired magical animal!" she explained. "Now he lives a nice, quiet life at the bottom of Adventure Lake. Charlie, these are my friends, Rachel and Kirsty."

"Hi, Charlie," the girls said together.

"We're searching for Bubbles, my magic seahorse," Rihanna continued. "We were wondering if you'd seen him."

Charlie looked thoughtful.

"Funny you should ask!" he replied in a booming voice. "I overheard

some of the other lake creatures talking about a new kid who's really friendly. I'll send out a message and ask if anyone's seen him today."

Rachel and Kirsty watched in fascination as Charlie began to hum a deep, low sound that created long ripples in the water. They waited. Then, after a moment, the water began to move again. This time, the ripples of sound were coming back toward them. Charlie cocked his head and listened.

"Bubbles was last seen near the middle of the lake," Charlie

announced. He pursed his mouth and
blew out a stream of shining bubbles.
"This underwater trail
will help you find him,"
he said, as the bubbles
floated ahead of
them. "But hurry,
before it disappears.
My magic doesn't last
long in the human world!"

"Thank you, Charlie!" Rihanna and
the girls called as they zoomed off.

The three friends swam quickly toward
the center of the lake, following Charlie's
magical trail. But, to their dismay, they
could see that the bright bubbles were
already fading away.

"Swim faster, girls!" Rihanna cried.
Panting hard, Rachel, Kirsty, and

Rihanna reached the middle of the lake just as the trail finally fizzled away. But there was no sign of Bubbles anywhere!

"Bubbles is such a friendly little seahorse," Rihanna said, as a large brown trout swam by lazily. "I'm sure he's made lots of friends here in the lake."

She turned to the trout. "Hello, there," Rihanna called. "Have you seen a seahorse around here?"

"I just saw one heading in the direction of Leggy Garden," the trout replied helpfully. "There were some really rude green creatures heading that way, too!"

"Goblins!" Rihanna gasped.

Rachel was just about to ask where Leggy Garden was—but then a hook with some bait on it plopped down into the water from overhead.

"As if I'm falling for that old trick!" the trout said scornfully. "Humans are so predictable!" He quickly swam away.

Kirsty glanced up and saw the bottom of a boat above them.

"Some of the campers must be fishing," she said. "We'd better move away so we don't get hooked!"

"But where's Leggy Garden?" Rihanna asked as they swam away from the boat.

"Let's head in the direction the trout came from," Rachel suggested.

As they swam through the water, Kirsty kept looking upward. She could see the bottoms of kayaks, canoes, and boats overhead on the surface of the lake. Suddenly she laughed.

"I know exactly where Leggy Garden is!" she announced. "Follow me!"

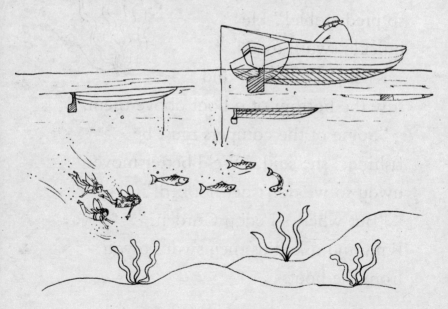

Quickly, Kirsty led Rachel and Rihanna toward the floating dock. Then Rachel and Rihanna burst out laughing, too. They could see the kicking legs of some of the campers as they swam around the dock!

"What a great name—Leggy Garden!" Rachel said, giggling.

"Girls!" Rihanna exclaimed in a dismayed voice. "I see goblins ahead! Quick, we have to make sure the swimmers don't spot them!" And she swam off, away from Leggy Garden.

Rachel and Kirsty rushed after Rihanna, toward the goblins. As they got closer, the girls were horrified to see that the goblins had formed a circle around a beautiful golden seahorse.

"It's Bubbles!" Rihanna cried.

Charlie to the Rescue

Bubbles was trying to swim out of the circle of goblins. But every time he darted forward, the goblins tried to grab him, making the circle smaller as they moved in closer.

"Bubbles can't escape, and I can tell he's getting tired!" Rihanna said anxiously as the little seahorse bobbed

around inside the ring of goblins. "What can we do?"

Just then, the big goblin glanced around and spotted them.

"Oh, hello!" he said, waving in a friendly way. "Sorry about this. We

don't like to come between good friends, but we have to do what Jack Frost says, you know!"

"Yes, it's a nasty job, but somebody has to do it!" added the smallest goblin with an apologetic smile.

"The goblins are even being nice to *us*," Kirsty whispered to Rachel.

"Bubbles' magic must be working overtime!"

"How on earth are we going to get Bubbles back?" Rachel wondered. Then an idea popped into her head. "Rihanna, do you think Charlie might be able to help us again?"

Rihanna's face lit up. "I'm sure he will!" she said eagerly. "I'll call him." She began to sing her little song once more.

The goblins turned to stare at
Rihanna, looking confused.

"What are you doing?" asked
the big goblin, as the water
around them began
to swirl with
sparkling bubbles.
"This is no time
for singing!"

"What's
happening?"
The third
goblin gasped.
"Why has
the water
become all
fizzy?"

"Well, a big old lake monster is on
his way here right NOW!" Rachel said

loudly. "And he won't be happy when he finds out you're trying to steal the magic seahorse. So you'd better let him go before the monster arrives!"

"Ha!" scoffed the smallest goblin. "You don't scare us! There's no such thing as a lake monster, and these bubbles are just a silly fairy trick!"

Laughing, he rushed forward, breaking the circle. This time, he managed to grab Bubbles and hang onto him.

"Hooray!" the

other goblins cheered. "Group hug!"

"OK, but I can't let
go of this seahorse!"
the smallest
goblin yelled.

As the
goblins
huddled
together
again, Charlie
appeared
through the
mass of sparkly bubbles.

"Charlie, the goblins haven't seen
you because they're too busy hugging!"
Kirsty whispered. "We need to get
Bubbles away from them. Can you be as
scary as possible?"

With a big grin, Charlie nodded. He

swam silently toward the goblins, who
were still congratulating themselves on
capturing the magic seahorse.

Charlie tapped the smallest goblin
on the shoulder with one of his huge
fins. . . .

The Gift of Friendship

The goblins turned around.

"BOO!" Charlie yelled in a thunderous voice that sent the water around them rippling in all directions.

The goblins' eyes opened wide in horror. They screamed loudly, and the smallest goblin instantly let go of Bubbles. Then all three goblins bolted through the water, disappearing into the distance at record speed. Rachel, Kirsty,

and Rihanna burst out laughing.

"Charlie, you were wonderful!" Kirsty
cried. She and Rachel both gave him a
big kiss on each cheek.

"Bubbles!" Rihanna called, her face
shining with delight. "Here I am!"

The golden seahorse bounced joyfully
through the water toward her. With
each flap of his fins, Bubbles shrank
a little. By the time he jumped into
Rihanna's arms, he was fairy-size
again! Rihanna gave him a hug, and
Rachel and Kirsty gathered around to
pet him, too.

"Girls, I need to take Bubbles back to Fairyland," Rihanna said. "But first, let's get you back to your canoe. I think the quickest way will be to ride on Charlie's back."

"Climb aboard!" Charlie called.

Rachel and Kirsty clambered onto Charlie's gray back, as did Rihanna, with Bubbles snug in her arms. Then Charlie swam through the water. Once again, they passed underneath the boats and canoes, and through Leggy Garden.

"None of our friends would believe that we are right below them, riding on the back of the lake creature with a fairy and a magic seahorse!" Kirsty whispered to Rachel, who laughed.

Very soon, they reached the canoe.

"Thank you, girls,"
Rihanna said, her
eyes sparkling.
"Because of you,
four of our beloved
magical animals are
back with their fairy
friends. I know we can
count on you to do your
best to find the others!"

"We will," Rachel and Kirsty
promised.

Rihanna smiled. "You two are very
lucky because you already have the
wonderful gift of friendship," she said.
"But now Bubbles will be able to spread
the magic of friendship even more.
Good-bye!"

"Good-bye," Rachel and Kirsty called.

Rihanna pointed her wand at the girls, and a burst of fairy magic sent them shooting up out of the water in a whirlpool of glitter. A moment later they were back in their canoe, and back to their normal size.

"Look, we're not even wet!" Rachel marveled. "Isn't fairy magic wonderful?"

"I'm so glad Bubbles is safe and sound." Kirsty sighed happily.

"Me, too," Rachel said. "A world without friendship would be like . . ." She stopped and thought for a moment. "Fairyland without magic!" Rachel finished, and Kirsty smiled and nodded in agreement.

RAINBOW magic

THE MAGICAL ANIMAL FAIRIES

Rihanna the Seahorse Fairy has
her magical animal back!
Now Rachel and Kirsty need to help . . .

Sophia
the Snow Swan Fairy!

Join their next adventure
in this special sneak peek. . . .

Into the Darkness

Kirsty Tate bit into a warm, sticky
marshmallow and smiled. Yum! It
had been another fantastic day at the
adventure camp where she and her best
friend Rachel Walker were staying for
a week. The sun was going down
and everyone was sitting around
a fire, singing songs and toasting
marshmallows. "I'm having such a

wonderful vacation," Kirsty said happily to Rachel.

"Me, too," Rachel agreed. Then she lowered her voice. "Especially with our new fairy friends!"

Kirsty smiled at her friend's words. She and Rachel shared an amazing secret. They had met lots of fairies and had shared all kinds of exciting adventures with them! This week, they were helping the Magical Animal Fairies find their lost animals because Jack Frost had stolen them. The girls had already helped the fairies find a young dragon, a magic black cat, a phoenix, and a seahorse . . . but there were still three animals left to return to Fairyland.

"Listen up, guys!" came a voice just then. Kirsty and Rachel turned to see

Trudi, one of the camp counselors, standing on a tree stump. "There's such a wonderful full moon tonight, we're going to take a night hike. I have something very special to show everyone. Can you get into pairs, please?"

The campers immediately hurried to pair up. Kirsty and Rachel went together, of course, and smiled at each other. They always had their most exciting times when it was just the two of them.

Two other counselors, Jacob and Lizzy, began passing out flashlights.

"Why are we going hiking in the dark anyway?" a girl named Anna wanted to know.

"Nature looks very different at night,"

Jacob told her. "All kinds of birds and animals come out that you don't see during the day. And the surprise waiting for you at the end of the trail will definitely make it worth the walk!"

When everyone was ready, the campers set off, flashlight beams bobbing across the grass. First they went through some dark woods. Because they heard strange scufflings all around them, Rachel and Kirsty kept close together.

Twigs snapped beneath their feet, and Kirsty stumbled on a long, twisted root. It was a relief when they came out from under the trees and into the open, where the moonlight lit the path and covered everything with a silver haze.

"It's so pretty," Rachel marveled as they walked alongside a bubbling stream. The moonlight glittered on the water as it rushed by.

"And look at that little swan!" Kirsty exclaimed. "It's so beautiful with the light reflecting on its white feathers — almost as if it were shimmering. . . ."

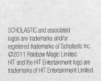